D1006847

ANDY SHANE
HERO at Last

Jennifer Richard Jacobson

illustrated by Abby Carter

CANDLEWICK PRESS

For Liz Bicknell and Kaylan Adair—my heroes
J. R. J.

For Carter, Samantha, and Doug
A. C.

H868 7270 7/12

First paperback edition 2011

The Library of Congress has cataloged the hardcover edition as follows:

Jacobson, Jennifer, date.
Andy Shane : hero at last / Jennifer Richard Jacobson ; illustrated by Abby Carter.
—1st ed.
p.   cm.
Summary: Andy wants two things very much—to win the contest for the
best decorated bicycle in the "Home Sweet Home parade" and to be a
hero—but his best friend Dolores stands in the way of at least one goal.
ISBN 978-0-7636-3600-5 (hardcover)
[1. Heroes—Fiction. 2. Parades—Fiction. 3. Bicycles and bicycling—Fiction.]
I. Carter, Abby, ill. II. Title.
PZ7.J1529Adh 2010
[E]—dc22   2008023737

ISBN 978-0-7636-5293-7 (paperback)

11 12 13 14 15 16 RRC 10 9 8 7 6 5 4 3 2 1

Printed in Crawfordsville, IN, U.S.A.

This book was typeset in Vendome.
The illustrations were done in black pencil and black watercolor wash.

Candlewick Press
99 Dover Street
Somerville, Massachusetts 02144

visit us at www.candlewick.com

CONTENTS

1
Four-Leaf Clovers

Andy Shane and Lucky Duck were sprawled in the grass in the shade of the high-school bleachers. Andy was looking for a lucky four-leaf clover. With luck, he thought, he was sure to get the two things he really wanted.

Every now and then he stopped searching and looked up at the high-school band. They were learning to march.

"Listen to the drum!" shouted the bandleader. "It will tell you what to do. *Boom*, lift one foot. *Boom*, lift the other foot. Match your feet to the drumbeat!"

The clarinet players bumped into the flute players. The trumpet players were so busy watching their feet, they forgot to play. *They'll need lots of practice,* thought Andy, *before they're ready to play in the Home Sweet Home Parade.*

Andy was going to be in the parade, too. He was going to ride his bike with all the other kids who wanted to win the contest for the best decorated bike.

"Hallooo," someone called.

Lucky Duck jumped up in record speed.

It was Dolores Starbuckle.

Andy knew that Dolores would

show up sooner or later. She'd

memorized all his favorite places.

"Did you find one?" she asked.

"Nope, not yet," said Andy.

"What do you need luck for?"

asked Dolores.

"To win the bike contest," said Andy.

"Oh, noooo," said Dolores. She
started looking for her own four-leaf
clover. "I told you *I'm* going to win the
contest. You can have second prize."

Now Dolores knew one thing that he wanted. But she didn't know the second thing—the thing Andy wanted even more than winning the bike contest.

What Andy Shane really, really, really wanted was to be a hero.

2
Ready and Willing

That evening, Granny Webb and Andy hiked to Swallow's Hollow. It was one of their favorite places in town. Together they sat on the edge of the small cliff and watched the swallows dip and swoop in and out of their nests.

"You were smart to bring a backpack,

Andy," said Granny Webb. "You never

know what you'll need when you explore."

Andy just smiled. He didn't tell
Granny that this wasn't an ordinary
backpack. This was his hero backpack.

There are some things you can plan, thought Andy. He had a plan for winning the bike contest. He was going to turn his bike into one of these awesome birds. The front of his bike would be a swallow's beak, and in the back there would be a feathered tail. He just had to figure out how to make wings that could flap in the middle. That was the part that would surely impress the judges.

But there were lots of things you couldn't plan. You couldn't *plan* to be a hero. You just had to be ready.

While Granny Webb scooted a little lower on the cliff to view the swallows through her binoculars, Andy unzipped his hero backpack and took a look at the things he'd collected.

He had:

1. Catnip for luring frightened kittens out of trees
2. A map for helping lost children find their homes
3. A rope to toss in case someone fell into the river
4. A flashlight in case someone fell down a hole
5. A camera for taking pictures of thieves or people who littered
6. Band-Aids for anyone who needed one

Andy had everything he needed to be a hero. Now he simply needed to be in the right place at the right time.

"Ack!" called Granny Webb from below.

"What?" cried Andy.

"I slipped on a rock."

"Hold on!" he shouted. "I'm coming!" Andy Shane pulled his rope from his backpack and tried to straighten it out.

But before he could get the rope

untwisted, Granny popped back up

to where he was standing.

"I forgot how slippery those rocks

can be," she said, brushing herself off.

"But I was going to rescue you!"
said Andy.

"Next time," said Granny Webb.

Andy and Granny collected swallow feathers that had fallen to the ground, and then they headed home.

On the way, they passed Dolores Starbuckle's house. She was in the driveway with her newly polished bike.

Blue, yellow, and white streamers flowed from the handlebars and in and out of the spokes of her wheels. The basket was covered in paper daisies, and inside was a tiny bike helmet that was also covered in daisies.

"You can't wear this!" said Andy, picking up the helmet. "It's way too small."

"That's for Myra," said Dolores. Myra was Dolores's cat. "She's going to ride in the front of my bicycle built for two."

"What a clever idea!" said Granny Webb. "Do you think she'll stay in the basket?"

Andy thought of Myra jumping from the bike and scurrying to the roof of the Merry Muffin Bakery on Main Street. Andy would race up the stairs, throw open the second-story window, and lure Myra to him with the catnip. Everyone would cheer as the cat with the flowered bike helmet crawled into his arms.

Andy reached down to pat Myra, who was rubbing up against Granny's legs. Myra hissed at Andy and reached out to scratch him.

Ack! Rescuing Myra would not be the way to become a hero after all.

Andy still didn't know how he would become a hero, but what he did know was this: if he didn't get working on his bike mighty quick, Dolores would win the contest for sure.

3

Bad Luck

The next day Andy rode his bike

to April's Craft Store to pick up

supplies. He picked out brown paint,

yellow paint, and glue.

On the way home he passed the
high school. The band was in the
parking lot, practicing for the parade.
A boy was pounding on the big bass
drum with a stick that looked like
a giant lollipop. The other band

members were quietly marching in place. Their feet were tapping with the *boom, boom, boom.* They were ready!

Andy zipped home so that his bike would be ready, too.

Granny helped Andy cut a tail out of cardboard, paint the background brown, and then glue some feathers on. "Tell me about the rest of the swallow," she said.

"I want long swallow wings in the middle—wings that can flap up and down. But I don't know how to attach them to my bike," said Andy.

"Maybe you should draw a picture," said Granny Webb.

Just as Andy and Granny were finishing up, Lucky Duck came into the barn to investigate. He was covered in grass and twigs.

"Where have you been?" asked Andy.

Lucky just sniffed the feathers.

"They're swallow feathers," said
Andy.

Lucky liked feathers. Before Andy
or Granny could grab his collar, he
rolled on the feathered tail.

"No, Lucky!" yelled Andy.

Lucky jumped up and ran from
the barn.

Andy knew better than to chase him.
There was nothing Lucky Duck loved
more than a game of tag. So Andy
sat down on the steps and waited . . .
and waited.

"Hallooo."

Not now, thought Andy. This was not
a good time to hear how wonderful
Dolores Starbuckle's bike looked.

Lucky came bounding over to say hello.

"He's covered in feathers," said

Dolores. "And brown paint."

"I know," said Andy. He tried to

pull a feather off, but it was stuck to

his fur. Lucky needed a bath.

Granny held Lucky in the bubbly
water. Dolores and Andy washed his fur.
The minute Granny let go of Lucky
to get a towel, he leaped from the
tub. He shook and spun, jumped
and rolled. Then he flew
out the door
and down the stairs.

"I'll get the feathers," said Dolores. She gathered all she could from the murky water and took them outside to dry in the sun.

Andy stayed and mopped the
water up off the floor, the counter,
and the walls. He was scrubbing the
dirt and paint out of the tub when
Granny walked in again.

"Why, Andy Shane," she said, looking around at the shiny bathroom. "You are my hero!"

Great, thought Andy. When it came to being a hero, this was NOT what he had in mind.

4
Saving the Day

He didn't think it could happen,

but on the day of the parade, Andy

Shane was ready.

On the back of his bike was a long swallowtail. The rest of his bike was wrapped in white strips of cloth to look like the belly of a swallow.

Andy sat on his bike.

Granny helped him slide wings—with paper feathers—onto his arms.

Then she helped him put on his helmet, which had been covered in papier-mâché to look like the head of a swallow—complete with beak. Andy and his bike made an impressive bird.

Andy saw Dolores where the bikes
were lining up for the parade.

"Don't come over here," yelled Dolores.
"I don't want you to scare Myra."

That was fine with him. He'd
already had dog trouble. He didn't
need cat trouble, too.

Andy realized that he had forgotten his hero backpack. He missed it.

The band started playing, and the parade began moving out of the parking lot and into the street.

First there were the important people in town, riding in convertibles.

Next came the Brownies,

the Girl Scouts, the Cub Scouts,

and the Boy Scouts.

The high-school band followed the Scouts. The flutes came first. Then came the clarinets and the saxophones. Next were the trumpets, and finally the drums. It was time for the bicycles to follow!

As Andy rolled into the street, he took one hand off the handlebars and waved his arm up and down. He wanted to look like a swallow in flight.

"Hey, look at that owl!" a little girl shouted.

An owl? thought Andy. *I look like an owl?* But this was the Home Sweet Home Parade, and everyone in town loved the birds at Swallow's Hollow! He wondered if he should have made a sign telling people what he was.

Suddenly the parade stopped. The music stopped. Even the *boom, boom, boom* of the drum couldn't be heard.

Folks continued to point and yell. Andy knew that they weren't all pointing at him. They were pointing out the bike that looked like a school bus, the bike that looked like a rosebush, and Dolores's bicycle built for two. So far, Myra was still in the basket, and she seemed to like the attention.

But not Andy! Even behind his bird's

beak, he felt shy. He put his head down.

That's when Andy saw something on the road—something that looked like a giant lollipop. Oh, no!

He leaned over on his bike to scoop it up, but his tires slid out from under him. *Crash!* Andy and his bike landed on the ground.

Several grown-ups asked Andy if he was okay and started to step into the street to help him.

But Andy jumped back onto his bike and steered ahead. He knew what he needed to do. He rode in front of the bike that looked like a school bus. He rode in front of the bike that looked like a rosebush. He rode in front of Dolores Starbuckle and Myra.

"Hey, Andy Shane," shouted Dolores. "*I'm* leading the bike parade!"

But Andy didn't stop. He could see the band up ahead, and they were confused. They didn't know if they should march forward or stay in place. They didn't know if they should play their instruments or rest. Where was the *boom, boom, boom*? They were looking backward. The bass drum wasn't beating.

Andy rode up to the bass-drum player and held out the drumstick.

The bass-drum player leaned over the snare-drum players.

Andy leaned over the snare-drum players, too. His bike wobbled, but it didn't fall.

The pass was made, the bass drummer started pounding, and the band played their next tune.

The crowd cheered.

When the parade ended, Andy didn't line up with the other bikes for the judging of the contest. His costume had been crushed when he fell over. But he didn't mind. He had a good feeling about the day just the same.

He gave Dolores a good-luck wave

as he went off to find Granny Webb.

He didn't see Myra, but she may

have been sleeping in the basket.

The next morning, just as Andy had cleaned all the white strips of cloth off his bike, Granny came out to show him something special.

It was the front page of the newspaper.

Town News

Hometown Hero
Andy Shane!

He had done it.

Andy Shane was a hero at last.